Snuggle Up, Little One

A Treasury of Bedtime Stories

Snuggle Up, Little One

A Treasury of Bedtime Stories

Little Tiger Press

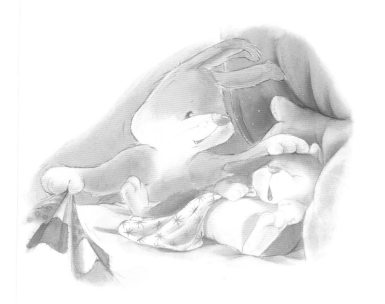

11

READY FOR BED!
by Jane Johnson
pictures by Gaby Hansen

37

I DON'T WANT TO GO TO BED!
by Julie Sykes
pictures by Tim Warnes

63

WHAT ARE YOU DOING IN MY BED?
by David Bedford
pictures by Daniel Howarth

89

HUSHABYE LILY

by Claire Freedman
pictures by John Bendall-Brunello

115

GOODNIGHT, SLEEP TIGHT!

by Claire Freedman
pictures by Rory Tyger

141

THE VERY NOISY NIGHT

by Diana Hendry
pictures by Jane Chapman

Ready for Bed!

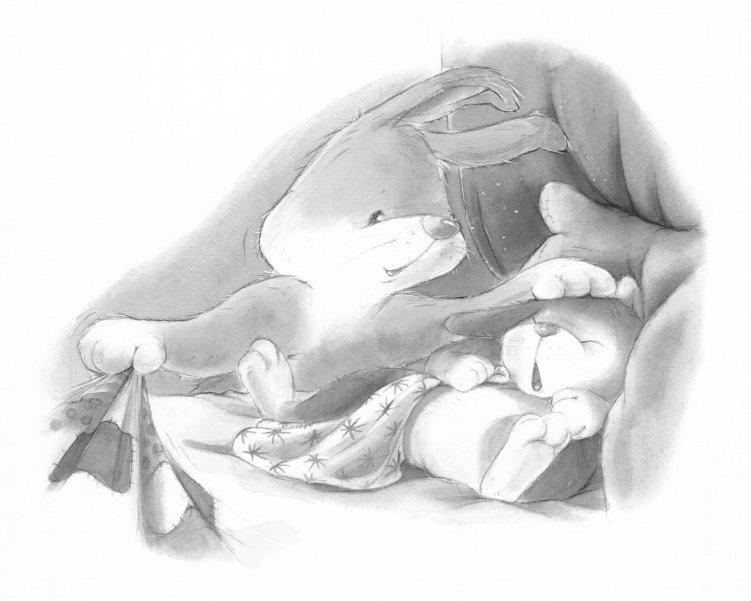

by Jane Johnson   pictures by Gaby Hansen

Mrs. Rabbit sighed when all of her children were tucked safely into bed. "Ah, peace and quiet at last," she said.

But Mrs. Rabbit had spoken too soon.

"Mommy, I can't sleep," said her youngest
child, Little Bunny, interrupting her first snore.

Mrs. Rabbit tried a gentle lullaby.
  "Hush-a-bye bunny on the tree top
  When the bough breaks, the cradle . . ."
Little Bunny's eyes began to close.
"Is my bunny sleepy now?" whispered
Mrs. Rabbit, so as not to wake the others.

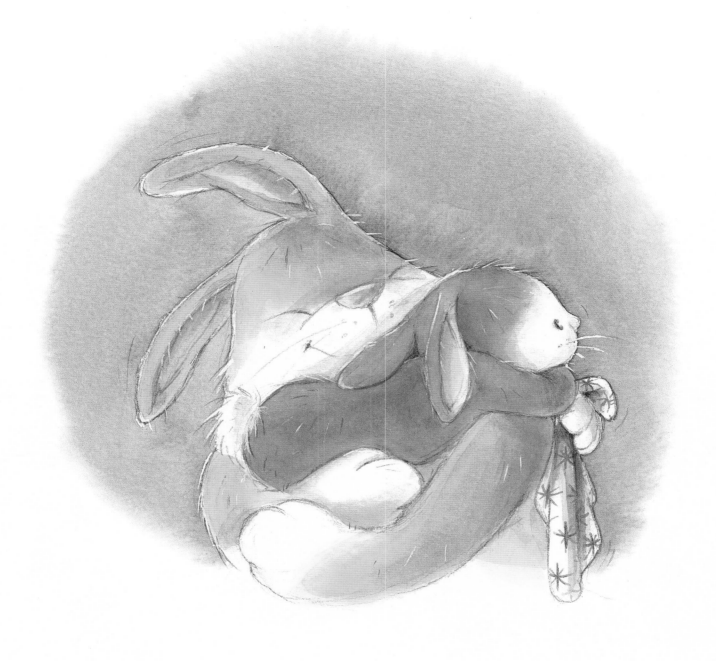

"No!" said Little Bunny. "I'm not sleepy at all."
He wanted to stay up all night long with his mommy.

Mrs. Rabbit tried a bubble bath.
"Rub-a-dub dub, my bunny needs a scrub,"
she laughed. "Who's my Little Bunny?"
"I am!" said Little Bunny, smiling sweetly.

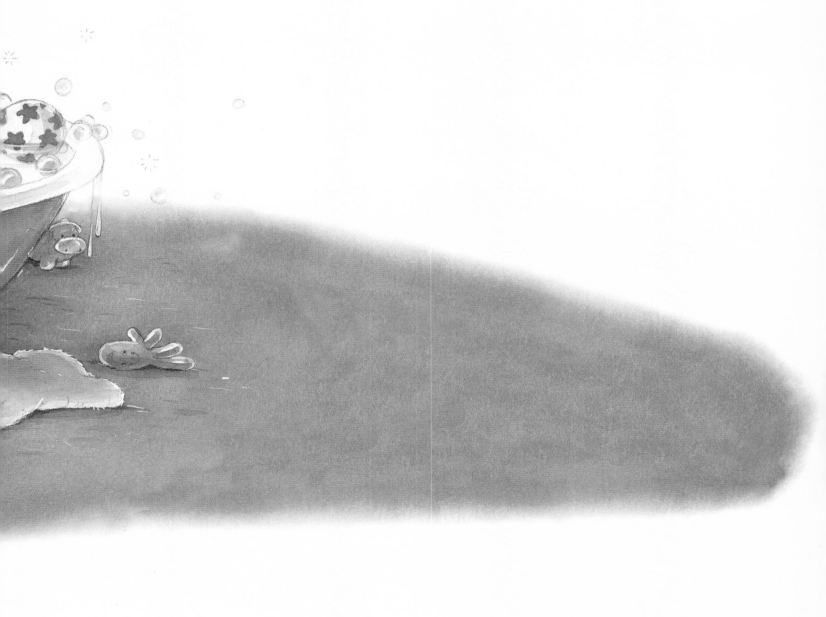

"Well now, darling, I think it's bedtime,"
Mrs. Rabbit said hopefully, drying his fur.

"No!" said Little Bunny. "It's not bedtime yet."

Mrs. Rabbit tried warm milk.

"Swirly, whirly, creamy white," she yawned.

"Time to cuddle and say 'Good night.'"

"Cuddle, yes! 'Good night,' no!" said Little Bunny.
He wanted to stay up with his mommy forever.

"Squeezy, huggy, snuggle up tight," he said happily.
"Am I the best little bunny
in the world tonight?"

"I love all my bunnies the same, sleepyhead," said Mrs. Rabbit.

"Then I'll never be ready for bed,"
said Little Bunny.

"What am I going to do with you?"
said his worn-out mother.
Little Bunny jumped up excitedly...

"Let's play bunny hops!"
said Little Bunny.

"Hoppity, hoppity, hop...

'round and 'round the room
till I..."

"Flop!" whispered Mrs. Rabbit.

"Zzz," snored Little Bunny.

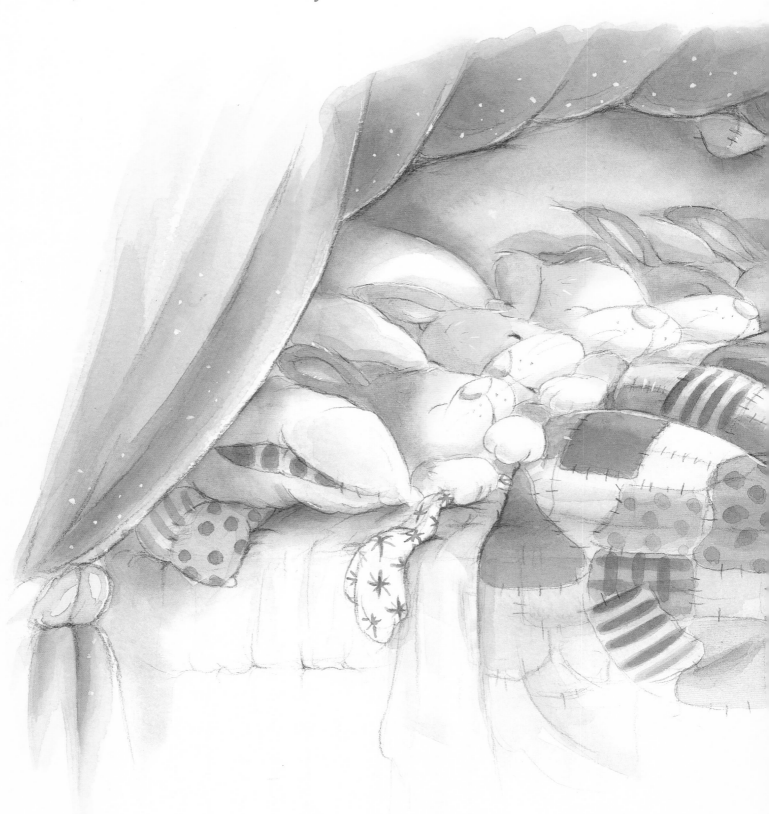

"Ah, peace and quiet at last,"
sighed Mrs. Rabbit.
"Even my youngest bunny
is asleep in bed."

Mrs. Rabbit flopped into bed,
but through her snores
she heard . . .

her second youngest bunny call out,
"Mommy, I can't sleep!"

I don't want to go to bed!

by Julie Sykes

pictures by Tim Warnes

Little Tiger did not like going to bed.
Every night when Mommy Tiger said,
"Bedtime!" Little Tiger would say,
"But I don't want to go to bed!"

Little Tiger wouldn't let Mommy Tiger clean
his face and paws, and he wouldn't listen to his bedtime story.
One night Mommy Tiger lost her temper. When Little Tiger
said, "I don't want to go to bed!" Mommy Tiger roared,
"ALL RIGHT THEN, YOU CAN STAY UP ALL NIGHT!"

Little Tiger couldn't believe his good luck.
He scampered off into the jungle before
Mommy Tiger could change her mind.

Little Tiger went
to visit his best
friend, Little Lion.

42

When he arrived, Little Lion was having his ears washed. "It's bedtime," growled Daddy Lion. "Why are you still up?"
"I don't want to go to bed!" said Little Tiger, and he skipped off into the jungle before Daddy Lion could wash his ears, too!

Little Tiger decided to visit his second best friend, Little Hippo.
He found him splashing in the river, having a bedtime bath.

"It's bedtime," bellowed Daddy Hippo. "Why are you still up?"
"I don't want to go to bed!" said Little Tiger, and he
scurried off into the jungle before Daddy Hippo
could give him a bath, too!

Little Elephant was Little Tiger's third best friend.
He went to visit him next.
Little Elephant was not out playing.
He was in bed, listening to his bedtime story.
"It's bedtime," trumpeted Mommy Elephant.
"Why are you still up?"
"I don't want to go to bed!" said Little Tiger,
and he bounced off into the jungle before
Mommy Elephant could put him to bed, too!

Little Tiger thought
he would go and find
Little Monkey, his fourth
best friend. But he found
Mommy Monkey first.
She put a finger to her lips and
whispered, "Little Monkey is fast
asleep. Why are you still up?"

"I don't want to go to bed!"
Little Tiger whispered back.
Quickly he tiptoed into the
jungle before Mommy Monkey
made him fall asleep, too!

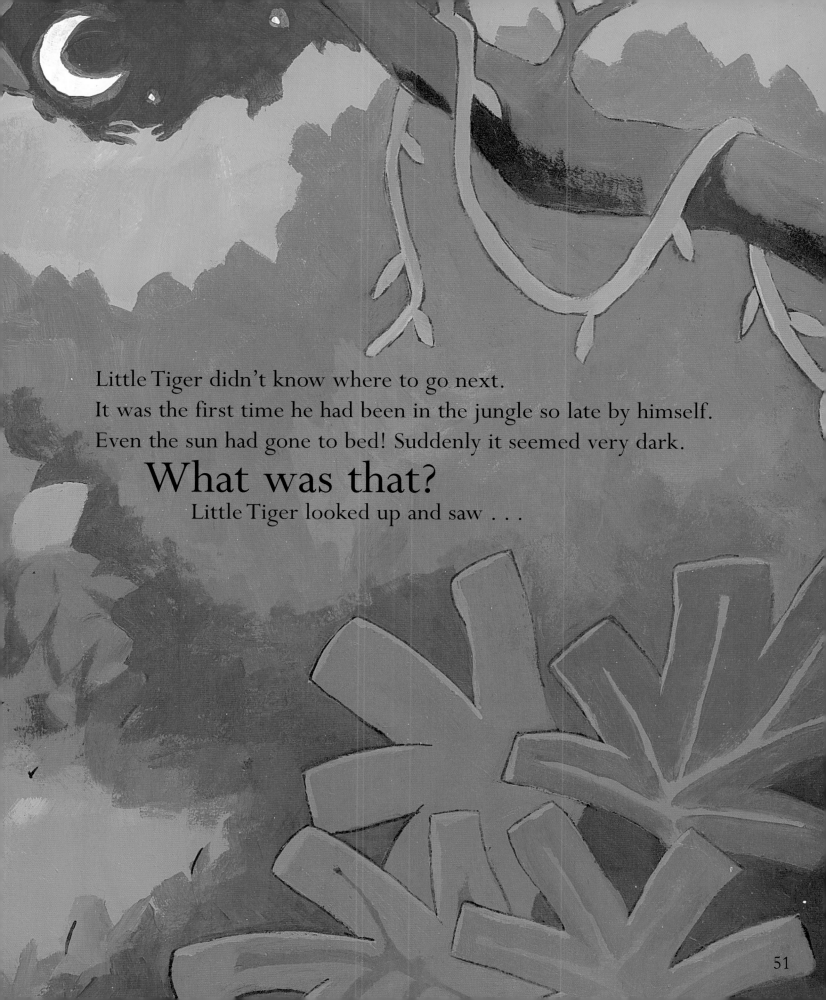

Little Tiger didn't know where to go next.
It was the first time he had been in the jungle so late by himself.
Even the sun had gone to bed! Suddenly it seemed very dark.

What was that?

Little Tiger looked up and saw . . .

51

. . . two very large yellow eyes
staring back at him!

The eyes belonged to a bush baby.
"Shouldn't you be in bed?" she asked.
"I don't want to go to bed," said Little Tiger bravely. "You haven't!"
"That's because I go to bed when the sun rises," said Bush Baby.

Little Tiger couldn't imagine going to
bed in the sunshine. He shivered and
thought how cold and dark it was in
the jungle at night.

"I'm going to take
you home," said Bush Baby. "Your
mommy will be worried about you."
"I don't want to go home! I don't want to
go to bed!" said Little Tiger. But he didn't want
to be left alone in the dark either.
So Little Tiger followed Bush Baby through the jungle.
He was glad of her big bright eyes to show him the
way back home.
"We're nearly there," said Bush Baby, as Little Tiger's
steps became slower and slower.

"I don't want to go to . . ."
said Little Tiger sleepily,
dragging his paws.

58

"Ah, there you are," said Mommy Tiger, "just in time for bed!"
"I don't want to . . ." yawned Little Tiger, and he fell fast asleep!

Mommy Tiger tucked him in and turned
to Bush Baby . . . but she wasn't there.
Bush Baby had disappeared into the jungle
before Mommy Tiger could tuck her in, too!

What Are You Doing in My Bed?

by **David Bedford**

pictures by **Daniel Howarth**

Kip the kitten had nowhere to sleep
on a dark and cold winter's night.
So he crept through a door . . .

. . . and curled up warm and
snug in somebody's bed.

Then out of the dark
Kip heard . . .

. . . whispers and hisses,
and soft feet padding
through the night.

Bright green eyes peered
in through the window,
and suddenly . . .

. . . one, two, three, four, five, six cats
came banging through the cat door!
They tumbled and skidded and rolled
across the floor, where they found . . .

... Kip!

"What are YOU doing in OUR bed?"
shouted the six angry cats.

"Your bed?" said Kip.
"But this bed's too small for
you. You'd never all fit!"

"Never fit?" said the cats.
"Just you watch . . ."

73

One, two, three cats curled up
neatly, head-to-tail . . .
then four, five, six cats
piled on top.

"See? There's no room
for you," they said.
"You'd never fit."

"Never fit?"
said Kip.
"Just you
watch . . ."

Tottering and teetering,
Kip carefully climbed on top.
"I'll sleep here," he said.

"OK," the cats yawned.
"But don't fidget or snore."
And they fell asleep in a heap.

But suddenly, a big, deep,
growly voice said . . .

"WHAT ARE YOU DOING IN MY BED? SCRAM!"

The cats scattered
round the room, but only
found hard, cold places
to sleep.

Harry the dog was comfy in his bed,
and he soon began to snore.

But then an icy wind whistled in through
the cat door, and Harry awoke
and shivered.

Kip whispered, "Follow me . . ."
and he quickly led six cold cats
across the floor . . .

. . . to the cozy bed.
   "We'll keep you warm,"
said Kip.

84

"You'll never all fit," chattered Harry.
"Never fit?" said Kip. "Just you watch . . ."

Kip and Harry snored right through the night
under their warm blanket of cats.

And they all fitted purr-fectly!

Hushabye Lily

by Claire Freedman
pictures by John Bendall-Brunello

Night time crept over the farmyard.
The moon rose higher into the darkening sky.
   "Are you still awake, Lily?" said Mother Rabbit.
"You should be fast asleep by now."
   "I'm trying, but I can't sleep," Lily replied.
"The farmyard's far too noisy for sleeping,"
                              and she picked up her ears.
                              "What's that quacking sound
                                 I can hear?" she asked.

"Hush now!" said Mother Rabbit. "It's only the ducks, resting in the tall reeds."

"Sorry, Lily!" called out a golden-eyed duck.

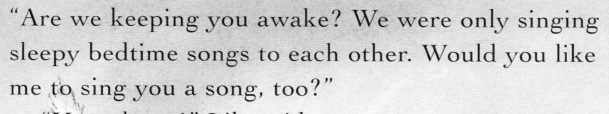

"Are we keeping you awake? We were only singing
sleepy bedtime songs to each other. Would you like
me to sing you a song, too?"

"Yes, please!" Lily said.

94

So the duck puffed out his chest, shook out his feathers,
and sang the most beautiful duck lullaby he knew.
"That was lovely!" sighed Lily, sleepily.
"Shhh!" whispered the duck. And without a sound, he
waddled away, back to the moonlit pond.

"Whooo, whooo!"
hooted the owl
on the barn roof.
    "Hush!" whispered
Lily's mother.
    The owl flew away,
high into the sky.

WHOO

WHOO

96

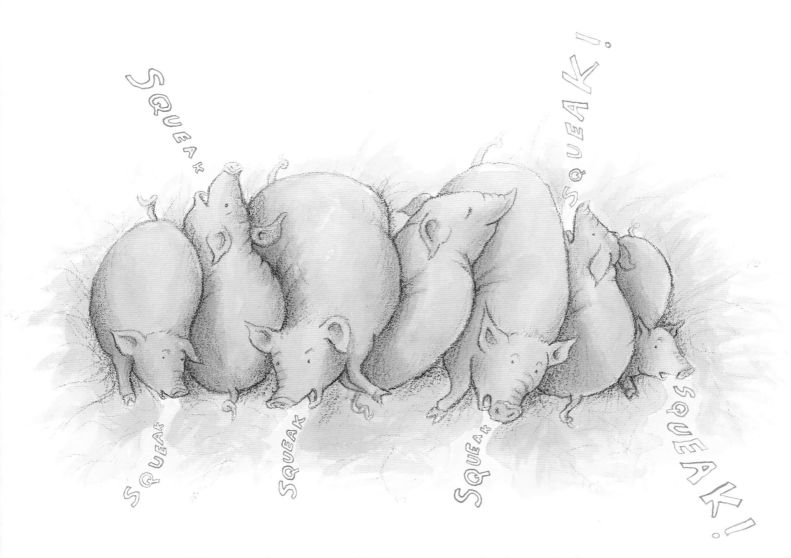

"Squeak, squeak," yawned the piglets,
nestling head-to-tail in the pigsty.
"Shhh!" sighed Mother Rabbit. "Hush!"
Sleepily, Lily closed her eyes . . .

. . . but before long she opened them again, and picked up her ears.

"What's that mooing sound I can hear?" she asked.

"Hush now!" said Mother Rabbit. "It's only the cows lowing in the cowshed."

"Sorry, Lily!" cried out a soft-eyed cow. "Are we keeping you awake? We were only telling each other bedtime stories. Would you like to hear a story, too?"

"Ooh, yes please!" said Lily.

So the cow told Lily her favorite sleepy bedtime tale.
"That was nice!" said Lily with a huge yawn.
"Shhh!" whispered the cow. And she lumbered back
to the old barn, as quietly as she could.

"Meow!" cried the farm cat,
huddling her kittens together.

"Hee-haw!" brayed the dreaming donkey,
turning in his sleep.

"Shhh!" sighed Lily's mother. "Hush now!"
Lily closed her eyes . . .

. . . but then she opened them again and picked
up her ears.

"What's that clucking sound I can hear?" she asked.

"Hush!" said Mother Rabbit. "It's only the hens
hiding in the haystacks."

"Sorry, Lily!" called out a bright-eyed hen.

"Are we keeping you awake? We were only collecting straw to make our beds more comfortable. Shall I find some straw for you, too?"

"I'd like that," said Lily.

So the hen brought back a beakful of straw,
and tucked it under Lily's head.
"That's cozy," said Lily, struggling to
keep her eyes open.
"Shhh!" whispered the hen, and she
crept off softly to the hen house, on tiptoes.

"Shhh!" hushed the ducks
to the rippling reeds.

"Shhh!" hushed the cows
to the leaves on the trees.

"Shhh!" hushed the hens
to the whispering wind.

"Hush now, Lily!" whispered Mother Rabbit,
and she snuggled up against her little one.
The moon hid behind the clouds.
All was quiet and still, until . . .

. . . down in the shadowy stable, a little brown foal
opened his eyes and picked up his ears.
"What's that whistling sound I can hear?" he asked.
"Shhh, go back to sleep!" his mother whispered.
"It's only little Lily snoring!"

Goodnight, Sleep Tight!

by **Claire Freedman**

pictures by
Rory Tyger

One night, Grandma was looking after Archie.

"Aren't you sleepy yet, Archie?" asked Grandma.

"No!" replied Archie. "I don't feel sleepy at all. I'm wide awake!"

Grandma sat down on the edge of Archie's bed.

"Do you have all your favorite friends to cuddle up with?" she asked. "They might help you feel sleepy."

"I've got Tiger and Rabbit," said Archie. "But where's Elephant?"

"Here he is," said Grandma, tucking him in nice and snug. "You cuddle up and you'll soon feel sleepy."

But neither Archie nor his little friends went to sleep.

"We're still wide awake, Grandma," he said.

"What about a nice warm milky drink?" said Grandma. "That makes me sleepy."

120

Archie drank every drop
of his warm milk. But he
didn't feel sleepy.
"I'm still wide awake,
Grandma!" he said.
"Please can we watch
the fireflies? That might
make me sleepy."

Grandma wrapped Archie in his cozy blanket and together they watched the dancing fireflies. Archie tried to count them but it didn't make him feel sleepy.

"I'm still wide awake, Grandma!" he said. "Can you sing me a lullaby, please? That might make me sleepy."

Grandma sang some of
Archie's favorite songs.
Archie closed his eyes and listened . . .
but he didn't feel sleepy.

"I'm still wide awake, Grandma,"
he whispered.

"I know, Archie," Grandma said.
"Let me rock you in my arms. That
will make you sleepy."

Grandma rocked Archie gently in her arms, all the way down to the apple garden and back. Archie felt safe and warm in Grandma's arms, but he didn't feel the tiniest bit sleepy.

"Grandma, I'm STILL wide awake!"
he said. "Will you tell me a story,
please? Listening to stories
makes me feel sleepy."

129

Grandma sat down comfortably, and
Archie snuggled up close to her.

She told him stories
about all the naughty
things his mommy
had done when
she was little
—just like him.

"Your mommy
never felt sleepy
at bedtime either,"
Grandma said.

Grandma carried Archie back inside.
She smiled a secret smile as she
remembered putting Archie's
mommy to bed when she
was little.

Grandma tucked Archie up in bed. She pulled the covers right up to his nose.

"I used to tuck your mommy up into bed, with the blankets pulled right up to her nose—like this!" said Grandma.

"Then I'd stroke the top of Mommy's forehead —like this," Grandma said.

Very gently she stroked the top of Archie's forehead.

"And I'd give Mommy a very special goodnight kiss," said Grandma.

Grandma gave Archie a special goodnight kiss.

"That's right, Grandma," said Archie
with a big yawn. "And then she says,
'Goodnight, sleep tight!'"
"That's right, Archie," said Grandma . . .

And before Grandma could even say "Goodnight, sleep tight", Archie was fast asleep!

The Very Noisy Night

by Diana Hendry

pictures by Jane Chapman

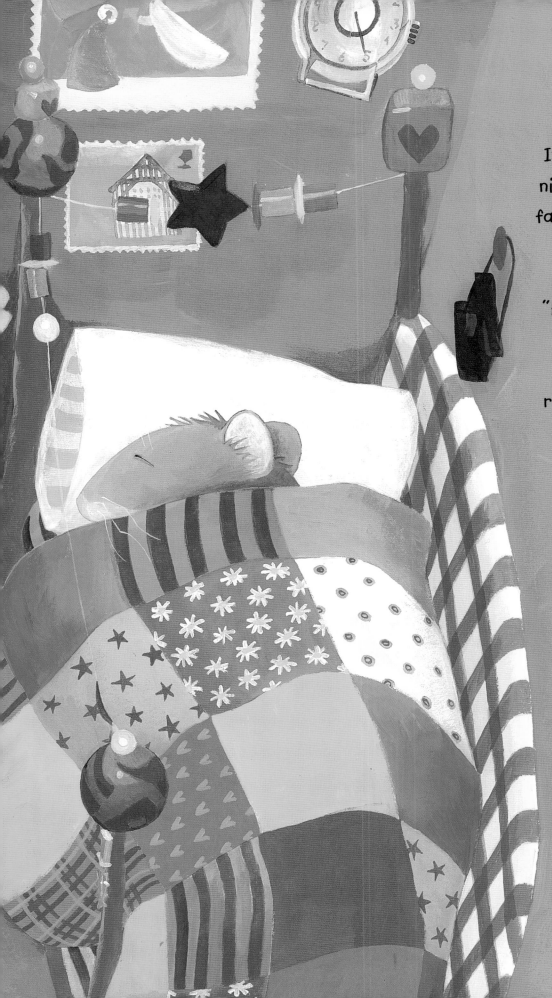

It was the middle of the night, and Big Mouse was fast asleep in his big bed. Little Mouse was wide awake in his little bed. "Big Mouse! Big Mouse!" called Little Mouse. "I can hear something rushing round the house, huffing and puffing."

Big Mouse opened one eye and one ear.
"It's only the wind," he said.

144

"Can I come into your bed?" asked Little Mouse.
"No," said Big Mouse. "There isn't room."
And he turned over and went back to sleep.

Little Mouse lay listening to the wind.
Then, suddenly, between a huff and
a puff, came a TAP TAP TAP TAP.

Little Mouse climbed out of bed, opened
the front door—just a crack—
and peeked out.

WHOOOSH! went the wind,
but there was no one outside.
"Big Mouse! Big Mouse!" called Little Mouse.
"I can hear someone tapping.
Perhaps there's a burglar on the roof."

147

Big Mouse got out of bed
and opened the bedroom curtains.
"Look," he said, "it's only a branch
tapping on the window. Go back to sleep."
"Can I come into your bed?"
asked Little Mouse.
"No," said Big Mouse. "You wriggle."

148

Little Mouse lay in his own bed and listened to the wind huffing and puffing and the branch tap-tapping—and someone calling,

"HOO-HOO! HOO-HOO!"

Little Mouse climbed out of bed again. This time he looked under it. Then he looked in the closet, and feeling very frightened he cried, "Big Mouse! Big Mouse! I think there's a ghost in the house, and it's looking for me. It keeps calling, who who? Who who?"

Big Mouse sighed, sat up
and listened. "It's only an owl,"
he said. "It's awake, like you."
"Can I come into your bed?"
asked Little Mouse.
"No," said Big Mouse. "Your
paws are always cold."
And Big Mouse pulled the
blanket over his head and
went back to sleep.

Little Mouse got back into his own bed and
he lay and listened to the wind huffing and puffing,
the branch tap-tapping, and the owl hooting.
But sssh! What was that?

"Big Mouse! Big Mouse!" he called.
"I can hear a drip. It's drip-dripping.
I think it's raining inside."
And Little Mouse jumped out of bed
and fetched his red umbrella.

155

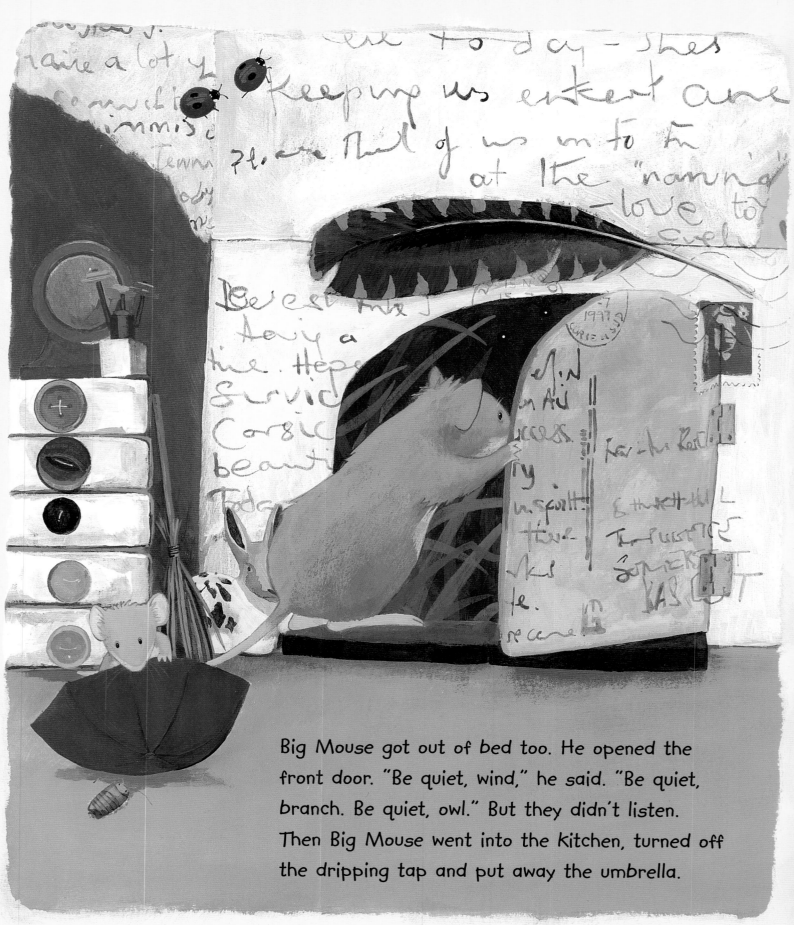

Big Mouse got out of bed too. He opened the
front door. "Be quiet, wind," he said. "Be quiet,
branch. Be quiet, owl." But they didn't listen.
Then Big Mouse went into the kitchen, turned off
the dripping tap and put away the umbrella.

"Can I come into your
bed?" asked Little Mouse.
"No, you're nice and snug in your own bed,"
said Big Mouse, taking him back to the bedroom.

Little Mouse lay and listened to the wind
huffing and puffing, the branch tap-tapping,
and the owl hooting. And just as he was beginning
to feel very sleepy indeed, he heard . . .

"WHEEE, WHEEE, WHEEEEE!"

"Big Mouse! Big Mouse!" he called. "You're snoring."

Wearily Big Mouse got up. He put his ear-muffs on
Little Mouse's ears. He put a paper-clip on his own
nose, and he went back to bed.

Little Mouse lay and listened to—n o t h i n g !
It was very, very, very quiet. He couldn't hear the
wind huffing or the branch tapping or the owl hooting
or Big Mouse snoring. It was so quiet that
Little Mouse felt he was all alone in the world.

He took off the ear-muffs. He got out of bed
and pulled the paper-clip off Big Mouse's nose.
"Big Mouse! Big Mouse!" he cried, "I'm lonely!"

163

Big Mouse flung back his blanket.
"Better come into my bed," he said.
So Little Mouse hopped in and his paws were cold . . .
and he needed just a little wriggle before
he fell fast asleep.

Big Mouse lay and listened to the wind huffing and
puffing and the branch tapping and the owl
hooting and Little Mouse snuffling, and very soon
he heard the birds waking up. But neither of
them heard the alarm clock . . .

BECAUSE THEY WERE
BOTH FAST ASLEEP!

Snuggle Up, Little One
A Treasury of Bedtime Stories
This edition produced 2004 for
BOOKS ARE FUN LTD
1680 Hwy 1 North, Fairfield, Iowa, IA 52556
by LITTLE TIGER PRESS
An imprint of Magi Publications
1 The Coda Centre, 189 Munster Road,
London SW6 6AW, UK
www.littletigerpress.com
ISBN 1 84506 169 1
Printed in China
2 4 6 8 10 9 7 5 3